지난밤 내 꿈에

지난밤 내 꿈에
Last Night, In My Dream

정한아 | 스텔라 김 옮김
Written by Chung Han-ah
Translated by Stella Kim

ASIA
PUBLISHERS

Contents

지난밤 내 꿈에
Last Night, In My Dream

외숙부는 외할머니의 사십구재를 예배식으로 치르
겠다며 우리를 집으로 불렀다. 사십구재 예배라는 게
대체 뭔지—내세로 가는 혼을 위한 제사를 기독교식으
로 어떻게 치른다는 것인지—의견이 분분했다. 버스
터미널에 내린 엄마를 차에 태우고 외가로 향하는 내
내 엄마는 외숙부를 욕했다. 장례 후 외할머니의 재산
내역을 확인한 외숙부가 엄마를 의심한다고 했다. 인
천의 협동농장 보상금이 문제였다. 숙부는 그것을 엄
마가 미리 가로챘다고 자못 확신하고 있었다.

"악착스럽기는. 자기는 이미 부자면서. 대체 무슨 욕
심이 그렇게 목 끝까지 찼다니."

Uncle told us to come to his house, saying that he wanted to perform the 49th day memorial rite for Grandma in a Christian way. Mom and I had different opinions regarding what a Christian 49th day memorial service would entail, considering the memorial rite was to send the spirit of the dead to the Buddhist land of bliss in the afterlife. I picked Mom up from the bus station and headed to Uncle's house, and she badmouthed her brother the entire ride. She said that he was suspicious of her after examining Grandma's assets. The main point of contention was the compensation Grandma had received from a collective farm in

"그러니까 부자지. 욕심 없이 어떻게 부자가 돼."

"넌 욕심이 없어서 부자가 아니고?"

"난 좀 어설프지. 우주는 간절히 원하는 사람의 소원만 들어준다고."

엄마는 뾰족한 눈으로 나를 보더니 땅이 꺼지게 한숨을 내쉬었다.

"사실을 알게 되면 전부 토해내라고 할 거다. 그러고도 남을 인간이야."

외숙부는 외할아버지가 돌아가셨을 때 대부분의 재산을 상속받았고, 외할머니가 거주중이던 강남 한복판의 아파트마저 용의주도하게 부부 공동명의로 바꿔놓았다. 그는 그것이 평생 시부모를 모시고 산 외숙모의 몫이라고 주장했다. 엄마는 펄펄 뛰었지만, 나는 한편일리가 있는 말이라고 생각했다. 누군가 내게 인철의 어머니를 모시는 대신 아파트를 준다고 한다면 조금도 고민하지 않고 손사래를 칠 것이다. 노인과 함께 사는 것은 쉬운 일이 아니다. 특히나 외할머니 같은 노인이라면.

외가에 도착한 우리에게 문을 열어준 사람은 외숙모

Incheon. Uncle was convinced that Mom had taken the money.

"So obnoxious," Mom said. "He's already rich. Why is he still up to his neck in greed?"

"That's how he got rich. You can't get rich without greed."

"Does that mean you're not rich because you have no greed?"

"I must not want it as much, I suppose. The heavens only grant the wishes of those who are desperate."

Mom glared sideways at me and let out an exasperated sigh. "If he finds out, he'll tell me to cough it all up. I wouldn't put that past him."

Uncle received most of the inheritance when Grandpa passed away, and he had even transferred the ownership of Grandma's apartment to himself and his wife. He claimed that his wife deserved the apartment, since she lived with Grandpa and Grandma and took care of them all her married life. Mom had a fit, but I thought he had a point. If someone told me that they'd give me an apartment if I promise to live with Incheol's mother, I would reject the offer without even a moment's hesita-

였다. 그녀는 어딘지 전과 달라 보였는데, 무엇 때문인지는 딱히 짚어낼 수 없었다. 잠시 후 나는 바뀐 것은 외숙모가 아니라 집안 풍경이라는 사실을 깨달았다. 외할머니가 돌아가신 후 한 달 반 동안 리모델링을 하고 가구와 전자제품까지 갈아치운 것이다. 이거 무슨 신혼집 같네. 엄마가 비틀린 얼굴로 웃으며 말했다. 거실에서 찬송가가 흘러나왔다. 교회에서 목사와 부목사, 성도 네 명이 와 있었다. 십여 년 전 외할아버지가 돌아가신 후 외할머니는 심신 불안정을 이유로 교회에 발을 끊었지만 외숙부는 여전히 그 교회에 다니고 있었다. 그는 힘깨나 쓰는 총무 장로라고 했다. 그래선지 장례 예배 날에도 교회에서 온 사람들이 사방에서 북적거렸다.

'사십구재 예배'는 특별할 것 없는 평범한 예배였다. 목사는 구원에 대한 설교 끝에 외할머니가 얼마나 신실하고 믿음직한 성도였는지를 거듭 강조했다. 할머니가 교회에 나가지 않은 십여 년은 없는 시절로 치는 것 같았다. 흘긋 엄마를 보니, 표정 없는 얼굴로 고개만 끄덕이고 있었다.

예배가 끝나자 교회 사람들은 차려둔 떡과 과일을 먹

tion. It is not easy to live with an old person, much less someone like my grandmother.

Auntie opened the door when we got to their apartment. She seemed somewhat different, but I couldn't tell exactly what about her had changed. A little while later, I realized that it wasn't my aunt who had changed but the interior of the apartment that was different. After Grandma had passed away, they renovated the apartment for a month and a half and even replaced all the furniture and appliances.

"My, my, looks like a couple of newlyweds will be moving right in," Mom said with a twisted grin on her face.

A hymn flowed out of the living room. The reverend, assistant reverend, and four congregants from the church were there. Over a decade ago, after Grandpa passed away, Grandma stopped going to church, citing mental and physical instability, but Uncle was still attending the very church. He was apparently a rather influential elder in charge of the church's general affairs. That was probably why there were so many peo-

고 떠났다. 외숙모도 약국에 갈 채비를 했다. 그들은 근방에서 제일 큰 약국을 운영하고 있었다.

"네 엄마와 조용히 할 얘기가 있으니 차에 가서 좀 기다릴래?"

외숙모가 집을 나가자 외숙부가 내게 말했다.

"그럴 필요 없어요. 애도 다 알아요. 엄마 살아 계셨을 때 한센인 집회에도 같이 갔었는걸요."

외숙부가 흠칫 놀라 나를 바라보았다. 나는 사실이라는 뜻으로 고개를 숙여 보였다.

"나가서 차에 있거라. 내가 불편해서 그래."

외숙부가 내게 간곡히 부탁했다. 그는 평생 외할머니의 병력을 감추고 싶어했고 그 사실을 외숙모에게까지 숨겼다. 나는 그런 그가 우습다고 생각했으나, 정작 하얗게 질린 얼굴을 보니 측은한 마음이 들었다. 외가에서 나온 나는 근방의 카페로 향했다. 엄마는 외숙부와 이야기가 끝나면 터미널까지 혼자 택시를 타고 가겠다고 했지만 차마 먼저 갈 수는 없었다. 문제가 된 보상금에 대해 일말의 책임감을 느꼈던 것이다.

외할머니가 한센인이라는 사실을 엄마가 내게 알려

ple from the church at Grandma's funeral service.

The 49th day memorial service was nothing special. At the end of the sermon about salvation, the pastor emphasized again and again how faithful and dependable Grandma had been as a congregant. It seemed as if he was pretending to have forgotten about those ten plus years that Grandma hadn't attended the church. I glanced over at Mom, and she was simply nodding along with a blank look on her face.

After the service, the people from the church ate the fruits and rice cakes Auntie had put out as refreshments and left. Auntie also got ready to head over to the pharmacy that she and Uncle ran—it was the biggest one in the neighborhood.

When his wife left, Uncle said to me, "Would you wait in the car while I talk to your mom? I need a word with her."

"No need," Mom said, "she knows everything. When mom was alive, she even went with her to a leprosy rally."

Uncle started and looked at me. I nodded once to confirm that what she said was true.

준 것은 열두 살 때의 일이다. 당시 엄마는 불행했던 결혼생활에 종지부를 찍었다. 한국에서의 사업 실패를 만회하고자 떠난 미국에서 또 한번의 파산을 경험한 뒤였다. 마지막 해에 아버지는 술에 절어 있었고, 걸핏하면 엄마에게 시비를 걸었다. 주먹질도 서슴지 않았다. 처음 때렸을 때는 깜짝 놀라 무릎을 꿇고 싹싹 빌더니 점차 뻔뻔해져서 나중에는 거칠 것 없이 개새끼처럼 굴었다. 엄마는 나를 데리고 도망치듯 집을 떠나야 했다. 한국으로 돌아오는 비행기에서 엄마는 아이처럼 울며 아버지가 그녀에게 저지른 온갖 만행을 읊어댔다. 그중 하나가 외할머니의 한센병력을 수치스럽게 여기고 내내 엄마의 약점으로 들먹였다는 것이었다. 그때 나는 한센병이 무엇인지도 몰랐다. 일종의 전염병이지만 전염력은 거의 없다는 것이 엄마의 설명이었는데 도대체 무슨 말인지 이해할 수 없었다. 다만 아버지가 외가를 재수 옴 붙은 집안, 이라고 싸잡아 멸시했던 까닭을 어렴풋이 깨달았을 뿐이다.

흔히들 외가라고 하면 따뜻하고 정감어린 추억을 하나둘씩 가지고 있지만 내 경우는 아니었다. 외할머니는 주변의 다른 할머니들과 달랐다. 말이 없고, 냉정하

"Wait in the car still," he pleaded. "I'm uncomfortable talking about it in front of you."

He'd wanted to hide Grandma's illness all his life; he never told his wife about it. I thought he was ridiculous for trying, but pity crept up from deep within my heart when I noticed how pale his face had turned. I left his apartment and headed to a coffeeshop nearby. Mom said that she'd take a cab to the bus station when she was done talking with her brother, but I couldn't possibly leave her. Because I was partly responsible for the compensation that became a problem between Mom and Uncle.

I was twelve when Mom told me that Grandma was a leper. At the time, Mom had put an end to her miserable marriage. It was after my father declared bankruptcy in the United States, where we had moved to after his business failed in Korea. In the last year of their marriage, my father lived drenched in alcohol, and he often picked fights with Mom. He didn't hesitate to use violence either. The first time he hit Mom, he started and knelt on the spot to beg for forgiveness. But he

고, 누구에게도 곁을 주지 않았다. 그렇다고 해도 미국에서 도망쳐온 우리를 그토록 매섭게 외면할 줄은 몰랐다.

"돌아가라. 돌아가서 임서방 비위 거스르지 말고 조용히 살아."

엄마는 부들부들 떨면서 할머니한테 대들었다. 새된 목소리로 죽어버리겠다고 소리를 지르고, 외가의 살림살이를 집어던지며 난동을 피웠다.

"봐라. 맞고 사는 여자들은 다 이유가 있다. 네가 이렇게 사람 속을 뒤집으니까 끝을 보는 거야."

외할머니의 입매가 비웃는 것처럼 일그러졌다. 그날 나는 외할머니를 절대로 용서하지 않겠다고 결심했다. 만에 하나 엄마가 외할머니를 용서하면 엄마도 용서하지 않겠다고 다짐했다. 하지만 그런 염려는 할 필요가 없었다. 그들은 내가 생각하는 것보다 훨씬 깊은 애증으로 뒤엉켜 있었다. 독한 말로 상처를 주고받으며 일년 내내 왕래하지 않는 것은 예사였다. 어쩔 수 없이 화해하고도 서로를 비난하다가 다시 싸움을 벌였다. 그들은 지긋지긋한 과거를 씹고 또 씹었다. 꼿꼿이 머리를 치켜드는 엄마만큼이나 단 한 번도 져주지 않는 외

grew brazen over time and acted like a real son of a
bitch toward the end. Mom took me and more or less
ran away from home. On the plane back to Korea,
she cried like a child and told me all about the terrible
things my father had said and done to her. One of them
was that he'd considered Grandma's disease shameful
and used to hold it over Mom's head throughout their
marriage. I had no idea what Hansen's disease was at
the time. Mom explained that it was a contagious disease that was rarely contagious, but that didn't make
any sense to me. I'd only become vaguely aware of the
reason that my father had disparaged Mom's family al-
together as a family of pathetic good-for-nothings.

Most people have at least one or two heartwarming memories of their mom's families, but that was not
the case for me. Grandma was not like other grand-
mothers. She was quiet and cold, hardly ever open-
ing her heart to others. Even knowing all that, I never
thought that she'd turn her back so cruelly to Mom and
me when we flew all the way back to Korea from the
United States.

"Go back," Grandma had said. "Go back and stay

할머니도 대단했다. 엄마는 스스로를 고아라고 불렀고, 그 말은 일부 사실이었다.

외할머니와 외할아버지는 한센인 수용소가 있던 섬에서 만나 결혼했다. 단종수술을 극적으로 피해 두 자식을 얻은 그들은 섬을 탈출해 한센인 격리촌인 협동농장에 들어갔는데, 무슨 이유에선지 엄마는 고아원에 보내고 외숙부만을 데려갔다. 추측건대 네 식구가 먹고살기 힘들기도 했을 것이고, 자식을 갖지 못한 주변 환우들에 대한 민망함도 있었을 것이다. 어쨌든 그들은 악착스럽게 돈을 벌어 십 년 만에 농장 생활을 청산했다. 서울로 오면서 엄마도 다시 불러들였다. 외할아버지의 가전제품 대리점 사업이 성공한 이후 엄마는 남부럽지 않은 십대를 보냈다. 재수 끝에 피아노 전공으로 음대에도 들어갔다. 이혼 후에 음악학원을 차릴수 있었던 것도 외가에서 지원해준 덕이었다. 하지만엄마는 어린 그녀를 버렸던 사람들, 그중에서도 특히아무 가책이 없어 보이는 외할머니를 용서하지 못했다. 엄마는 고아원에서 보낸 시간이 자신을 망쳐놓았다고 말했다. 인간에 대한 불신과 환멸을 그곳에서 다배웠다고 했다. 차라리 온 식구가 섬에서 거지꼴을 겨

quiet, try not to get on your husband's nerves."

At Grandma's words, Mom had lashed out at her, shaking in rage. She shrieked at the top of her lungs that she was going to kill herself and threw a fit, grabbing whatever was in her reach and hurling it.

"See?" Grandma had said, her lips twisted into something like a sneer. "There's a reason some women get beaten by their husbands. He's done what he's done to you since you're acting this way."

On that day, I vowed never to forgive Grandma. And I vowed not to forgive Mom either if she ever forgave Grandma. But I need not have worried about the latter. Mom and Grandma were entangled in a love-hate relationship that was much more deep-seated than I could ever have imagined. They hurt each other with venomous words and often went an entire year without seeing each other. They would be forced to make up for one reason or another, then they would criticize each other and fight again. They kept on mulling and brooding over the infernal past again and again. Mom raised her head up defiantly every time, but Grandma never relented—they were a match made in heaven. Mom

우 면하고 살아가는 편이 더 좋았을 거라고도 했다. 외할머니는 들은 척도 하지 않고 콧방귀를 뀌었다.

엄마가 어떻게 생각하든, 외가가 소유한 협동농장 땅은 네 식구를 먹여 살렸다. 전국에 있는 한센인 협동농장 중에서도 그곳은 특히 입지가 좋은 편이었다. 그런데 어느 날 협동농장의 대표가 말도 안 되는 헐값으로 땅을 모 기업에 팔아버렸다. 나중에야 그가 뒷돈을 받은 사실이 드러나면서 지난한 법정 다툼이 시작되었다. 땅을 잃은 한센인들은 소유권을 되찾기 위해 집회를 벌였다. 외숙부는 외할머니가 집회에 참여하는 것, 소송에 뛰어드는 것을 강하게 반대했다. 기사에 실리거나 사진이라도 찍힐까봐 두려웠던 것이다. 동네에 외할머니의 병력이 알려져 약국이 망하면 다 같이 죽는 거라는 그의 말에 외할머니는 수긍했다. 외숙부는 장례식이 끝난 뒤에야 외할머니가 한센인 연합회의 가장 적극적인 일원이었다는 사실, 기나긴 소송 끝에 보상금을 받아 연금보험에 가입했다는 사실, 그리고 이미 총 수령액의 절반을 써버렸다는 사실을 알아냈다. 속았다는 사실을 안 외숙부가 느낀 것이 분노일지 슬

called herself an orphan, and she was right, in a way.

Grandma and Grandpa met on a leper colony island and married. After dramatically avoiding sterilization and giving birth to two children, they escaped the island and went to live in a collective farm for lepers. For some reason, my grandparents sent my mom to an orphanage and only took my uncle with them. I presume that it must have been difficult to feed a family of four, and possibly they felt bad for having two children when others at the farm couldn't have any. In any case, they worked furiously to make money and ended their farm life after ten years. They moved to Seoul and brought Mom back from the orphanage. Grandpa's home appliance store flourished, and Mom spent her teenage years without want for anything. She studied for another year after graduating high school and enrolled in college to major in piano performance. She was able to start a small music academy after her divorce, all thanks to the financial support she received from her parents. But Mom could not forgive the people who had abandoned her when she was a mere baby—particularly her mother who seemed to have no remorse. Mom said

품일지 궁금했다.

외숙부가 쫓고 있는 돈, 외할머니가 매달 수령한 보험금은 내가 가져갔다. 오백여만원씩 삼 년 칠 개월 동안, 이억이 넘는 액수였다. 내가 원한 것은 아니었으나 내 앞에 왔을 때 나는 거절하지 않았고(거절할 수 없었다), 그럼으로써 외할머니와 관련된 여러 가지 이슈에 얽히게 되었다. 돈이란 그런 것이다. 받으면 뭔가를 내주게 되어 있다. 그러니 섣불리 받아서는 안 된다. 하지만 돈이 없을 때, 말라붙었을 때 인간은 이성적인 판단을 하기가 힘들다. 묻고 따지고 할 겨를이 없다. 삼 년여 전의 내가 그랬다.

당시 나는 의정부의 연립주택 투룸에서 무직자 애인과 살고 있었다. 인철이 처음부터 무직자였던 것은 아니다. 입시학원 국어 강사였던 인철은 희곡을 쓰고, 무대 조명 아르바이트를 하고, 때로는 야학에 나가서 아이들을 가르쳤다. 시간에 쫓겨 뛰어다니면서도 그 모든 일을 즐겼다. 같은 학원에서 일하지만, 미국에서 유년을 보낸 이력 하나로 어쩔 수 없이 영어 강사가 된 나와는 달랐다. 그는 서른다섯 살이 되기 전에 극작가로

that the time she spent in the orphanage ruined her. That was where she became disillusioned about humans and learned to distrust them. It would have been better for all four of us to have lived on the island even if they would have been steeped in poverty, she said. Grandma brushed all that off with a snort.

Whatever Mom's feelings about the farm was, the plot of land within the farm owned by my grandparents was what put the food on the table for their family of four. Of all the collective farms for Hansen's patients around the country, theirs had a particular advantage for its location. But one day, the head of the collective farm sold the land to some company for a penny. Later people found out that he had taken bribes, and thus began a long and tedious legal battle. Hansen's patients who lost their lands held rallies to reclaim their ownership of the farmlands. Uncle was dead set against Grandma attending the rallies or taking part in the collective lawsuit. He was afraid that she might be mentioned or have a photograph taken of her and published in newspapers. He said that if the people in their

데뷔하겠다는 야심을 품고 있었고, 이를 위해 오래전부터 적금을 붓고 있었다. 아무 일도 하지 않고 일 년간 글만 쓸 수 있는 돈. 그는 그 돈으로 자기 삶의 새로운 광맥을 발견할 수 있으리라 믿었다.

우리는 사귄 지 얼마 되지 않아 같이 살기 시작했다. 서른이 넘었지만 둘 다 빈털터리라(나에게는 낭비벽이, 그에게는 가난한 부모가 있었다) 보증금이 천만원도 되지 않는 월셋집을 얻었고, 마트에서 산 물건으로 살림을 채웠다. 친구들이 하나둘 결혼해서 큰 집과 자동차를 사고, 아이들을 낳아 키우는 것을 봐도 부럽다는 생각은 들지 않았다. 결혼은 처음부터 우리의 계획에 없었다. 그렇게 살기 위해 감수할 것들을 상상하기만 해도 경악스러웠다. 지금이 좋다고 우리는 입을 모아 말했다.

엄마의 생각은 달랐다. 결혼은 문제가 많은 제도지만 동거는 더 나쁘고, 인철 같은 가난한 남자에게 꼬여 후자의 삶으로 떠밀리는 것은 최악이라고 했다. 나는 엄마의 반응에 놀랐다. 그녀는 언제나 자신의 삶, 자신의 연애가 더 중요한 사람이었기 때문이다. 엄마는 내 진로나 미래에 별 관심이 없었다. 낮에는 학원 일로, 밤

26

neighborhood found out that she had been a Hansen's patient, his pharmacy would lose all customers and that would be the end of their family. Grandma agreed. Only after her funeral did Uncle find out that Grandma was *the* most active member of the Association of Hansen's Disease Patients, that after a long legal battle she finally received compensation, which she used to sign up for an annuity, and that she'd already spent half of the benefit. I wondered whether Uncle felt angry or sad when he found out that he'd been duped.

The money that Uncle was searching for, the monthly payments Grandma received from her annuity—I took it. Over five million won a month for exactly three years and seven months, the total came to more than 200 million won. I hadn't wanted it, but when the money fell into my lap, I didn't, or actually couldn't, refuse. And so I was entangled in various issues involving Grandma. That's how money works—if you take it, you have to give something back in return. That is why you shouldn't be rash with taking someone's money. But when you have no money, when you're all dried up, it's impossible to make logical decisions. You don't have

에는 데이트로 거의 매일 집을 비웠다. 나는 우리가 모녀보다 자매 관계에 가깝다는 생각을 하며 자랐다. 그러니 인철에 대한 엄마의 반대에 냉담해질 수밖에 없었다. 나의 동거 사건이 그녀 삶의 주축이라 할 수 있는 불안과 허영에 옷을 입혀 무대에 올릴 기회가 되었던 것일까? 엄마는 몰래 학원까지 찾아와 인철을 만났다. 돈봉투라도 줬나 하면 그건 아니고, 남편 없이 자식을 키운 인생사와 하나뿐인 딸을 향한 애끓는 심정에 대해 늘어놓은 후 간곡히 헤어져달라고 부탁했다. 나는 인철이 아닌 동료 강사에게 그 이야기를 들었다. 인철은 그 앞에 앉아 고개도 들지 못했다고 했다.

나는 엄마에게 화를 내지 않았다. 그저 부끄러웠을 뿐이었다. 엄마에 대한 나의 감정은 늘 그랬다. 엄마와 조용히 끊어지고 싶었다. 영원히 연락할 수 없는 곳으로 사라지고 싶었다. 하지만 그럴 수 없었다. 그러기에 나는 그 여자를 너무 오래, 많이 봤다. 미국에서 아버지라 불린 그 개새끼한테 곤죽이 되도록 맞던 것, 나를 데리고 도망치면서 땀에 젖은 손을 덜덜 떨던 것, 어린 딸앞에서 말의 명과 암을 구분하지 못하고 토해내던 상처의 붉은 살들—그런 기억들이 고스란히 내 안에 남

the luxury to ask questions. That was how I was about three years ago.

At the time, I was living in a cheap two-room townhouse in Uijeongbu, right outside of Seoul, with my then-unemployed boyfriend. Incheol wasn't always unemployed. A Korean teacher at a cram school that helped prepare students for the annual university entrance exam, he wrote plays, worked part-time lighting gigs, and occasionally taught night school classes. He was busy rushing about everywhere as he was always pressed for time, but he enjoyed every moment of his work. He was different from me, who was working at the same cram school as an English teacher for no other reason than that I could speak English because I had spent my childhood in the United States. He aspired to debut as a playwright before the age of 35, and he had been saving up for a long time to make his dream come true. Enough money to spend an entire year doing nothing else but writing. He believed that he would be able to start a new chapter of his life with that money.

Not long after we started dating, we moved in to-

아 있었다. 나는 그 여자를 저버릴 수 없었다.

　내가 인철과 헤어지지 않는다는 사실을 받아들인 뒤 엄마는 그를 없는 사람 취급했다. 차라리 그 편이 나았다. 인철은 그후 일 년간 두문불출하며 희곡 작업에 매달렸다. 하지만 몇 군데 공모전의 예심만 통과했을 뿐 연거푸 낙선의 고배를 마셨다. 나는 그에게 다음 기회가 있을 거라고 위로했으나 솔직히 아무래도 상관없으니 하루빨리 돈벌이를 시작하기를 바라는 마음뿐이었다. 생활비 통장이 진작 바닥을 보인 상황이었다.

　인철은 손을 털고 일어나 다시 일을 구했다. 그런데 뜻대로 되지 않았다. 전의 입시학원은 물론 동네 작은 보습학원에서도 그를 원하지 않았다. 일이 꼬이기 시작하니 이상하게 계속 꼬였다. 주말마다 조명 아르바이트를 했던 소극장은 불황으로 도산했고, 십 년 넘게 활동비를 받고 봉사해온 야학은 신설된 청소년 센터의 관할로 넘어가면서 문을 닫게 되었다. 인철은 공황 증상으로 약을 먹어가며 건설 현장을 돌아다녀 일당을 받아왔다.

　나는 그에게 더 쉬라고 말할 수 없었다. 오 년째 함께 살아온 연립주택 집주인이 바뀌면서 집을 나가달라는

gether. We were both in our 30s and penniless (I was a spendthrift; he had poor parents). So we rented a tiny apartment with a small deposit of less than 10 million won, and we filled our apartment with stuff we bought from warehouse stores. Even when my friends married one after another and bought big apartments and cars and had babies, I didn't envy them a bit. Marriage wasn't part of Incheol and my plans. It was appalling enough to imagine the things we would have to give up and put up with to live that way. We are great as we are, we said in unison.

Mom thought differently. She said marriage was a problematic institution, but cohabitating was worse, and being forced into the latter because of a poor man like Incheol was the worst. I was surprised by her reaction. Her own life and her own love life were always more important to her than anything else. When I was growing up, she wasn't very interested in my career or future. She was barely home, working at her music academy during the day and going on dates at night. I grew up thinking that Mom and I were more like sisters than a mother and a daughter. So I couldn't help

통보를 받은 참이었다. 우리가 가진 돈으로는 더 낮은 곳으로 내려갈 수밖에 없었다. 그전까지는 가난이 우리의 선택이라고 생각했지만, 선택의 여지가 없는 상황으로 내몰리자 여유랄지 정서랄지, 비참해지지 않기 위해 끝까지 붙잡고 있던 줄이 끊어져버린 느낌이었다.

우리의 관계도 몇 차례 위기를 맞았다. 가장 심각했던 시기는 월경이 몇 달째 없던 때였다. 임신에 대한 공포감으로 숨이 막힐 지경인 내게 인철은 유리 반지를 내밀며 청혼했다. 나는 그것이 아주 질 낮은 농담이라고 생각했다. 하지만 인철은 진심이었고, 나에게는 그 진심이 질 낮은 농담보다 더욱 나빴다.

산부인과 진찰 결과 나는 임신이 아니라 자궁의 혹을 떼어야 하는 상황이었다. 어렵게 하루 휴가를 내서 수술 스케줄을 잡고 입원 준비를 하면서 처음으로 인철과 크게 다투었다. 전부 돈 때문이었다. 돈이 다 말라버렸고, 설마 했지만 정말 한 방울도 남지 않았고, 병원에서 신용카드의 남은 한도액을 다 써버리면 그때부터 손가락만 빨면서 한 달을 버텨야 할 상황이었다. 두려움에 무릎이 꺾이는 나와 달리 인철은 태평하기만 했다. 그가 정말 태평한 것이 아니라 태평한 척하는 것이

but be indifferent to her objection. Perhaps my cohabitation incident clothed her anxiety and vanity, which were the two main pillars of her life, and gave them an opportunity to shine on stage. Without me knowing, Mom came to the cram school where I worked and met with Incheol. She didn't give him an envelope full of money to tell him off, like typical mothers who object to their children's marriage do in Korean TV dramas. Instead, she told him a heart-breaking story about her life as a single mother and how much affection she had for her only daughter—me—and pleaded with him to break up with me. Incheol said nothing to me about meeting my mother; I heard about it from another colleague. Incheol apparently couldn't even hold up his head high during their meeting.

I wasn't angry at Mom. I was embarrassed. That was the dominant emotion I felt toward her. I wanted my ties with my mom to be severed quietly. I wanted to disappear to a place where she could never contact me. But I couldn't—I'd seen too much about her for much too long to do that. I'd seen her beaten to a pulp by that son of a bitch I used to call father back in the United

란 사실을 알면서도 나는 그를 맹렬히 비난했다. 넌더리를 내며 유리 반지를 집어던졌다. 인철은 집을 나가서 며칠간 들어오지 않았다. 우리는 그렇게 끝날 수도 있었다.

하지만 인철은 수술 전날 돌아왔다. 그가 돌아왔다는 사실에 내가 얼마나 안도했는지, 지금도 생생히 기억한다. 그는 아무 일도 없었다는 듯 병원에 갈 채비를 하더니, 수술 전 금식을 앞두고 있던 내게 뭘 먹고 싶으냐고 물었다. 우리는 땀을 뻘뻘 흘리며 감자탕을 먹었다. 자꾸 눈가가 뜨거워졌지만, 나는 꾹 참고 밥도 볶아 먹자고 말했다.

수술 당일 엄마를 부르자는 인철의 제안을 나는 단호하게 거절했다. 그래서 마취에서 깨어나 엄마를 봤을 때 순간 꿈인가 했다.

"여기 1인실은 없니?"

엄마는 누구에겐지 모를 물음을 던졌다. 인철이 허둥지둥 원무과로 달려간 뒤 나는 1인실로 옮겨졌다. 추가금은 엄마가 계산했다. 내 상태를 보고도 엄마는 별로 놀라지 않았다. 학원에 연락했다가 내 소식을 들었다고 했다. 잠시 후 의사가 들어와 수술 경과에 대해 말해

States, her hands shaking and covered in sweat as she took me and ran away from him, the bloody flesh of wounds she vomited in front of her young daughter, unable to distinguish between the light and the darkness of her words—these memories were all there inside me. And I couldn't abandon her.

After accepting the fact that I wouldn't break up with Incheol, Mom treated him like he didn't exist. It was better that way. After that, Incheol devoted himself to writing plays at home for a year. Unfortunately he only made it through the preliminary round of several competitions and suffered a series of failures. I comforted him by telling him that he'd have another chance, but honestly I didn't care. I only hoped that he'd get back to making money as soon as possible. Our bank account was already showing bottom.

Incheol stopped writing plays and started looking for work again. But things didn't go as expected. Neither the cram school where we had worked together before, nor small local tutoring schools wanted him. Once things started going awry, everything else followed suit. The small theater where Incheol had a part-time light-

주었다. 엄마가 의사에게 궁금한 것들을 묻는 동안 인철은 투명인간처럼 벽에 붙어 있었다.

금세 돌아갈 줄 알았던 엄마는 해 질 무렵 가방에서 편한 옷을 꺼내 갈아입었다. 아예 밤을 새울 작정으로 온 것 같았다. 괜찮으니 그만 가보라고 해도 듣지 않았다. 결국 주변을 서성이던 인철이 집에 돌아갔다.

저녁에 보호자 식사를 주문한 엄마는 밥을 먹으면서 내내 맛이 없다고 불평했다. 음악학원 아르바이트생에게 수시로 전화를 걸어 이러저러한 일로 짜증을 냈다. 아홉시부터 드라마 두 개를 연달아 보았다. 그러면서 누군가와 오 분 단위로 메시지를 주고받았다. 병실의 불을 끈 뒤에도 휴대폰 진동이 계속 울렸다. 나는 종일 굶은데다 수술 부위가 욱신거려서 한마디 말을 할 힘도 없었다. 밤새 피를 쏟아 패드가 흥건해졌다. 새벽에 간호사가 와서 그것을 갈아주었다.

다음날 아침 일찍 나는 인철에게 메시지를 보냈다. 인철은 시키는 대로 커피와 빵을 사 들고 병실로 왔다. 엄마는 반가워하며 커피를 받아들었다.

"애, 나 빵은 안 먹어. 글루텐 덩어리 뭐가 좋다고."

"그럼 커피만 드세요. 식사는 집에 가서 하시고요. 이

ing job every weekend went bankrupt during the recession, and the night school where he had been teaching for over a decade in exchange for a small sum of money was shut down, as it came under the supervision of a newly established youth center. Taking medication to relieve his panic attacks, Incheol went to work at construction sites and brought home a day's pay for a day's work.

I could no longer tell him that it was okay not to work. Our landlord had sold the townhouse where Incheol and I had been living for five years, and the new landlord had just told us to pack our bags. With the meager sum of money we had, we had no choice but to go somewhere worse. Until that moment, we thought that poverty was our choice; but when we were forced into a situation without a choice, it was like the thin thread of composure or calm that we had been holding onto in an effort not to fall into misery had finally snapped.

Our relationship also hit several reefs. The most serious one was when I hadn't menstruated for several months. When I was at the point of suffocating from the fear that I might be pregnant, Incheol proposed to

제 그만 가도 돼요."

"그런데 얘가 왜 이렇게 어제부터 자꾸 가라고 난리야."

"불편해서 그러지. 엄마도 불편하잖아."

엄마는 서운한 듯 나를 빤히 보더니 요란하게 옷을 툭툭 털고 일어나 가겠다고 했다. 엄마가 떠난 뒤 협탁 위에 봉투가 놓여 있는 것을 보았다. 인철이 봉투를 들고 쫓아 나갔다. 엄마는 멀리 가지도 않았다. 병실 앞 의자에 우두커니 앉아 있다가 인철과 함께 돌아왔다.

"이 돈 뭐예요?

"뭐긴 뭐야. 주는 거지."

"우리도 돈 있어요."

마음에도 없는 소리를 하려니 혀가 꼬이는 것 같았다.

"그래도 그냥 받아둬."

나는 엄마 앞에서 봉투에 든 돈을 꺼냈다. 오백십이만 삼천사백원. 백원짜리 동전이 시트 위로 떨어져 데구루루 굴러갔다. 엄마가 잠자코 그것을 내려다보다가 입을 열었다.

"나도 받은 돈이라 그래."

"누구한테요?"

me with a glass ring. I thought it was an uncouth joke. But Incheol was sincere, and to me, his sincerity was worse than an uncouth joke.

After a checkup at the obstetrician, I learned that I wasn't pregnant but had to have a fibroid removed from my uterus. I barely managed to take a day off to schedule the surgery, and while preparing for hospitalization I got into a huge fight with Incheol for the first time. It was all because of money. The money we had was all dried up—we were literally, completely broke. Once I used up the remaining limit on my credit card at the hospital, we would have to go an entire month just sucking on our thumbs. My knees were buckling in fear, but unlike me Incheol seemed carefree. Although I knew he wasn't really carefree and that he was only pretending, I lashed out at him. Telling him I was fed up, I flung the glass ring into the air. Incheol walked out on me and didn't come home for several days. We could have split up like that.

But Incheol came home the day before my surgery. I vividly remember the relief I felt when he had returned. As if nothing had happened, he got ready to go

"외할머니한테. 인천 협동농장 보상금으로 연금보험을 들어놨던 모양이야."

나는 입을 다물었다. 내 표정을 본 인철이 슬그머니 병실을 나갔다.

"엊그제 찾아와서 현금으로 주더라. 앞으로 매달 줄 거래. 왜 주냐고 하니까 유산이라고."

"할머니 안 돌아가셨잖아요?"

"그러니까 말이다. 영문을 모르겠어."

"어쨌든 엄마 돈이에요. 저는 필요 없어요."

"글쎄 그게."

엄마는 화장을 안 한 얼굴로 나를 멀거니 보다가 말했다.

"협동농장 보상금이라는데 그걸 내가 어떻게 받아 쓰니. 그래서 널 주는 거야. 너에게는 쓸모가 있을 테니까."

외할머니와 외할아버지가 악명 높은 섬에서 나와 협동농장에 들어갈 수 있었던 것은 그들에게 얼마간의 돈이 있었기 때문이었다. 외할머니가 전남편에게서 훔친 돈. 그 남자는 외할머니가 한센병에 걸렸다는 사실을 알게 되자 독약을 건네며 조용히 죽으라고 권했다.

to the hospital and asked me what I wanted to eat before the operation. We sweated profusely as we shared the steamy pork bone stew. I felt hot tears welling up my eyes, but I held them in and said we should stir fry some rice with the stew.

I flat out rejected Incheol's suggestion to call Mom on the day of my surgery. So when I woke up from anesthesia and saw her, I thought that I was dreaming.

"Don't they have private rooms in this hospital?" Mom asked no one in particular.

After Incheol rushed to talk to a hospital administrator, I was moved to a private room with a single bed. Mom paid the additional cost. She wasn't very surprised to see me in the condition I was in. She said she'd heard about me when she contacted the cram school where I worked. Moments later, the doctor came in and told me about my progress. While Mom asked him questions, Incheol stood glued to the wall like an invisible man.

I thought she would head home soon, but at sundown Mom took out comfortable clothes from her bag and changed into them. It seemed as though she

외할머니는 돌쟁이인 딸을 두고 그 집에서 쫓겨났는데, 아무리 생각해도 그대로는 죽을 수 없었기에 돈과 패물을 빼돌렸다. 남자는 얼마 지나지 않아 도둑맞은 것을 알아차렸겠지만 외할머니를 쫓아 한센인들의 섬에 들어올 배짱은 없었을 것이다. 그렇다면 그녀의 딸은 어찌되었을까. 엄마는 외할머니가 그 딸로 인해 평생을 죄의식 속에 살았고, 또다른 딸인 자신에게 더욱 인색하게 굴었다고 했다. 그러지 않았다면 자신을 고아원에 보내놓고 어떻게 세 식구만 오붓하게 농장에서 돼지와 닭을 키우며 살아갈 수 있었겠냐는 것이었다.

솔직히 말해서 나는 그 모든 내용에 관심이 없었다. 피부가 녹아내리는 병에 걸려서 사회로부터 배척당했던 한 무리의 사람들. 그중 한 명이 내 조상이라고 해서 뭐 어떻단 말인가? 아무리 생각해도 별 감흥이 없었다. 그런데 정말 그런 일이 있을 수 있나? 실질적인 전염력을 가지지 않음에도 오해와 억측만으로 린치를 당하고, 격리 수용 당하고, 죽는 날까지 가족들을 만나지 못하는 그런 일이 가능한가? 역사에는 그렇다고 나와 있다. 그러니까 나는 그들 무리의 후손으로, 상황이 나아지지 않았다면 저 산골 농장에서 바깥세상에 한 번 나

had come to stay with me all night. She didn't listen to me even when I told her that I was okay and that she should go home. Eventually, Incheol went home instead.

In the evening, Mom ordered a hospital meal for caregivers, and while she ate, she complained how tasteless everything was. She kept on calling the part-timer at her music academy and yelled at her for various reasons. From nine o'clock she watched two TV dramas in a row. The entire time, she exchanged texts with someone every five minutes. Even after she turned off the lights in the room, her cell phone continued to vibrate. Having not eaten anything for that entire day and feeling a throbbing at the surgery site, I had no strength to tell her off. The disposable bed pad was soaked with the blood I shed all night. At dawn, a nurse came to change it.

Early in the morning, I texted Incheol. As I'd instructed him, he arrived at the hospital with coffee and some pastries. Mom only welcomed the cup of coffee.

"Hon, I don't eat pastries. There's nothing good about those masses of gluten."

와보지도 못한 채 살아갔을 수도 있다. 으스스한 분위기의 미국 드라마 소재로나 어울리는 이야기였다.

하지만 그 모든 게 뜬구름 같은 얘기로 들린다고 해도 매달 오백십이만 삼천사백원은 달랐다. 의미심장한 액수였다. 그 깊이와 너비가 손에 닿을 듯했다.

"줄 것 줬으니 난 이제 간다."

엄마는 인철에게 인사도 하지 않고 병원을 떠났다. 나는 인철과 마주앉아 봉투에 담긴 돈과 그 출처에 대해 이야기했다. 한센인이라는 말에 그는 오호, 하는 표정을 지었다. 그것이 전부였다.

"그래서 매달 그 돈을 주신다는 거야?"

"외할머니와 엄마의 마음이 바뀌지 않는 한."

인철은 멍하니 허공을 보았다.

"왜 그래?"

그는 혼잣말을 하듯 중얼거렸다.

"내가 어제 무슨 꿈을 꿨나 생각하는 중이야."

그날 밤에는 좀처럼 잠을 이룰 수 없었다. 나는 보호자 침대에서 몸을 둥글게 말고 잠든 인철의 등을 오랫동안 조용히 바라보았다.

급박한 상황이 되면 우리도 상대에게 독을 내밀며 죽

"Then just have your coffee," I told her. "And go home and eat. You can go now."

"Why do you keep telling me to go home?"

"Because I'm uncomfortable. You're not comfortable here either, are you?"

Looking sad, Mom stared at me, then loudly brushed off her clothes and stood up, saying that she'd go. After she left, I noticed an envelope on the side table. Incheol grabbed the envelope and ran after her. Mom hadn't even gone very far; she was sitting quietly on the bench across from my room. She followed Incheol back into the room.

"What is this money?" I asked her.

"What do you mean what is this money? I'm giving it to you, obviously."

"We have money," I said, feeling my tongue twist as I spat out the words I didn't mean.

"Take it, still."

As she stood watching, I took the money out of the envelope. Five million one hundred and twenty three thousand four hundred won. A hundred won coin fell onto the bedsheet and rolled down. Mom quietly stared

으로고 권할 수 있을까.

외할머니와 외할아버지는 섬 안에 있는 교회에서 만났다고 했다. 외할아버지는 한센인이 아니었으나 교회에서 종 치는 일을 하며 자란 전쟁고아였다. 그는 신앙심이 깊었고 모든 것을 하나님과 연관 지어 생각했다. 한센인 부인을 맞는 것 역시 기도 끝에 내린 결단이었다.

외할머니는 매일 새벽 네시에 일어나서 외할아버지와 같이 기도회에 나갔다. 그녀는 교회에서 가장 많은 일을 하는 권사였고, 예배와 행사의 주축이었다. 할머니가 없으면 교회 식당이 돌아가지 않는다고들 했다. 외할아버지가 세상을 떠난 뒤 할머니는 그 모든 수고와 노력을 돌연 그만두었다. 교회 쪽으로는 발길도 하지 않았다. 외할머니는 신을 믿지 않았다. 다만 외할아버지를 위해 그 모든 일을 했던 것이다.

다음날 아침 나는 간호사에게 걷기 운동을 좀 하라는 지령을 듣고 산부인과 병동을 한 바퀴 돌았다. 어디서 웃음소리가 들려 쫓아가봤더니 한 떼의 산모들이 유리창 너머로 신생아들을 보고 있었다. 우리는 똑같이 풍

at the coin before finally saying, "I'm giving you the money because it just fell into my lap."

"How?"

"Your grandmother gave it to me. Apparently she signed up for an annuity with the compensation she received for the collective farm in Incheon."

I closed my mouth. Seeing the look on my face, Incheol slipped out of the room.

Mom continued, "She came to see me a couple days ago and gave me the money in cash. Apparently, she'll give me the money every month. I asked her why and she said it was my inheritance."

"But she's not even dead."

"I know. I don't know why she's doing this."

"But, in any case, it's your money, Mom. I don't need it."

"The thing is…" Mom paused. Staring at me with no makeup her face, she said, "It's the compensation she received for the collective farm suit, so how could I possibly take it? That's why I'm giving the money to you. Because it'll be of use to you."

The reason Grandma and Grandpa were able to es-

성한 원피스 환자복을 입고 있었다. 그들은 아기를 낳았고, 나는 물혹을 떼어냈다. 슬그머니 그들 틈에 서서 잠든 아기들을 구경하고 있는데 엄마에게서 전화가 왔다.

"퇴원했니?"

"아직. 이따 오후에 의사 선생님 보고 퇴원할 거예요. 인철이가 같이 있잖아. 걱정하지 마요."

엄마는 잠시 뜸을 들이더니 다시 물었다.

"그애한테 돈에 대해서 뭐라고 말했어?"

나는 엄마가 궁금한 게 뭔지 알아차렸다.

"사실대로 말했지. 엄만 그게 뭐 대단한 비밀이라고. 인철이는 횡재한 사람처럼 굴던데. 나한테 뭐라고 했는지 알아? 어제 내가 무슨 꿈을 꿨더라? 이러더라니까."

엄마는 어이가 없다는 듯 힘없이 웃었다. 그런데 뭔가 후련한 기색이었다. 엄마는 알았다고, 됐다고, 몸을 잘 회복하라고 격려한 뒤 전화를 끊었다.

퇴원 후 버스를 타고 집에 돌아오는 길에 인철과 나는 정말로 매달 오백만원이 들어온다면 뭘 하고 싶은지에 대해 이야기를 나누었다. 나는 제일 먼저 여행을

cape from the notorious island and join the collective farm was that they had some money. It was the money Grandma had stolen from her ex-husband. When that man learned that Grandma had the Hansen's disease, he handed her poison and told her to quietly off herself. Grandma was kicked out of their house, and she was forced to leave her one-year-old daughter behind. But no matter how hard she thought about it, she couldn't die that way, so she pocketed his money and jewelry. The man must have realized that she'd stolen from him, but he probably didn't have the guts to chase her into the leper island. What happened to her daughter? Mom said that Grandma lived her entire life with guilt about her first daughter hanging over her head, and that must have made her act nasty to her other daughter—my mom. Because how else could Grandma and Grandpa send their daughter to an orphanage and live only with their son? A cozy little family of three, raising pigs and chickens on the farm.

Frankly speaking, I didn't care about any of that. A group of people who were shunned by society because of a skin-melting disease. One of them was my ances-

가고 싶다고 했다. 아무 계획 없이 무작정 떠나는 여행. 시간과 돈을 재거나 따지지 않고, 돌아올 날짜 같은 것도 염두에 두지 않고, 발길 닿는 대로 떠돌아다니다가 마음이 내키면 짐을 풀고 한없이 늘어지는 여행. 카페든 식당이든 아이들이 있는 곳은 무조건 피할 것이다. 깨끗하고 조용한 어른들의 세계로만 떠다닐 테다. 아이들의 괴성, 고자질, 토라짐, 낄낄거리는 웃음소리는 전부 끝이다. 지긋지긋한 아이들!

인철이 놀란 눈으로 나를 보았다.

"난 아이들이 좋은데……"

그는 잠시 망설이다가 입을 열었다.

"그렇지만 매달 오백만원이 생긴다면, 취직에 대한 압박이 없다면…… 좀더 집중해서 글을 써보고 싶어. 딱, 일 년만 더."

나는 고개를 끄덕였다.

"약속된 수입만 있다면 뭘 해도 좋겠지. 느지막하게 일어나서 땅콩을 수북하게 까먹고, 고양이랑 시시덕거리며 놀고, 밤새 다리 밑에서 춤을 추는 거야. 그래도 누가 뭐랄 거야?"

"외할머니께 감사하네. 이렇게 즐거운 생각은 정말

tor, so what? No matter how much I thought about it, I didn't feel anything. But could such a thing really happen? Was it possible for a group of people to be lynched, quarantined, and banned from seeing their families their entire lives? History said, yes, it happened. So, as a descendant of a member of that group, if the situation hadn't improved, I might have lived in that farm deep in the mountains without ever seeing the outside world. It was a story you might come across in an American TV show with an eerie vibe.

But, even if all of that sounded surreal, the monthly stipend of 5,123,400 won was different. That was a significant amount. Its depth and breadth seemed within my reach.

"Since I've given you what I came to give you, I'm going to go now." Mom left the hospital without saying goodbye to Incheol.

I sat face to face with Incheol and told him about the money in the envelope and where it came from. Hearing the word "Hansen's disease," he raised his eyebrows in an expression that seemed to say, "Oh, I see." That was all.

오랜만이잖아."

인철이 웃으며 말했다.

"그렇지만 적은 액수도 아니고, 부담이 되는 것도 사실이야. 잘 생각해보고 거절해도 좋아."

집 근처 정류장에서 지팡이를 든 노인이 버스에 오르자, 기사는 한참 동안 차를 출발하지 않고 기다려주었다. 잠자코 그 모습을 지켜보던 인철이 입을 열었다.

"외할머니…… 힘든 삶을 살아오셨겠다."

"그래, 맞아."

나는 인철의 말에 수긍했다.

아무 대가 없이 매달 들어오는 돈, 그것이 정말 가능할까? 가능했다. 매달 10일이 되면 꼬박꼬박 돈이 들어왔다. 인철은 부담이 된다고 했지만 무슨 헛소리, 나는 조금도 부담되지 않았다. 애타게 매달 10일만 기다렸다. 그 돈은 정말 유용하게 잘 쓰였다. 월세를 올려 이사하고도 넉넉히 남았다. 나는 학원으로 복귀하지 않았다. 매일 집에서 햇빛에 떠다니는 먼지를 바라보며 유유자적했다. 소고기와 치킨과 떡볶이와 체리와 자몽을 마음껏 사 먹었다. 새 운동화를 사고, 필라테스를 하러 다니기 시작했다. 인철과 용돈을 나눠 쓰면서 그 역

He then asked, "So she's going to give us that money every month?"

"As long as she and my grandma don't change their minds."

Incheol stared into the air.

"What's wrong?" I asked.

He murmured, as if to himself, "I'm thinking about what dream I must have had last night to deserve such a fortune."

I had a hard time falling asleep that night. For a long time, I quietly gazed at Incheol, who was curled up and asleep with his back to me on the cot next to my bed.

If we were ever forced into a pressing situation, would we come to the point of giving each other poison and telling each other to die?

I'd heard that Grandma and Grandpa met at a church on the island. Grandpa wasn't a Hansen's patient, but he was a war orphan who grew up ringing bells at the church. He was a pious man and thought about everything in relation to God. Taking a Hansen's patient as his wife was also a decision he made after long prayers.

시도 글을 읽고 쓰는 데 종일 시간을 들일 수 있었다.

우리는 저녁을 먹다가, 텔레비전을 보다가, 밤거리를 산책하다가 충동적으로 여행을 떠났다. 마치 어린아이들의 놀이 같았다. 누군가 이야기를 꺼내면 곧바로 기차 티켓을 예매하고, 짐을 꾸려서 문을 열고 나서는 데까지 걸리는 시간을 단축시키는 놀이. 기술이 숙달되자 한마디 말이 현실이 되는 데까지 채 오 분도 걸리지 않았다. 이런 식의 삶이 어떻게 가능한가 하는 질문을 우리는 더이상 하지 않았다. 그것은 우리의 이해로는 가능하지 않은 이상한 은총 같았다. 그 끝에는 분명 대가를 지불한 늙은이가 있었고, 우리는 매달 10일이 되면 그에 대해 이야기하지 않을 수 없었다. 질병의 숙주라는 오명, 시민권의 박탈, 격리 생활, 인격 비하와 모멸, 무작위로 행해진 낙태와 생체실험에 대해서. 대화는 종종 침묵 속에서 끊어졌고, 인철은 몸을 떨었다. 그는 홀로 남아 글을 썼다. 캄캄한 밤중에 스탠드를 켜고 등을 둥글게 말고 앉아 끝없이 무언가를 썼다.

다음해에도 인철은 신춘문예와 공모전에 낙선했다. 그나마 한 군데서는 최종심에 올랐으나 '발군의 문장이 무색할 만큼 낡은 이야기'라는 악평을 받았다. 인철

Grandma woke up at four every morning and went to church with Grandpa. She became a church elder who did the most work at the church, and she played a key role in worship services and other church events. People said that the church cafeteria wouldn't run properly without her. After Grandpa passed, however, she stopped all the church work at once. She even stopped going to church. Grandma didn't believe in God. She'd only done all that for her husband.

The next morning, a nurse told me to walk around and get some exercise, so I took a stroll around the maternity ward. When I heard laughter, I followed the sound and noticed that it was coming from a group of mothers watching their newborn babies through the glass. We were all wearing the same one-piece patient gowns that hung loose on our frames. But they had given birth to babies, while I had a fibroid removed. I was standing quietly among them, watching the sleeping babies, when I got a call from Mom.

"Are you home yet?"

"Not yet. I'll be discharged after I talk to the doctor in

은 이제 그만하겠다고 말했다. 할 만큼 했다고, 더이상 아쉬움이 없다고, 모두에게 고맙다고 했다. 마치 수상 소감이라도 말하는 것 같았다. 우리 둘 다 울 뻔했다. 그때 심사위원 중 한 사람에게서 연락이 왔다. 인철의 희곡을 무대에 올리고 싶다고 했다.

인철은 서울의 제일 큰 극장에서 첫 작품을 올렸다. 마지막날 엄마도 극장에 왔다. 연극이 끝난 뒤 우리는 다 같이 저녁식사를 하러 갔다. 한센인 여인이 주인공으로 나오는 연극에 대해서 엄마는 한마디도 하지 않았다. 희곡은 몇 살부터 썼는지, 한 작품을 쓰는 데 며칠이나 걸리는지, 하루 몇 시간 책상에 앉아 있는지 그런 시답잖은 것만 물어봤다.

엄마는 그날 유난히 많은 양의 음식을 먹었다. 특별히 준비한 빈티지 보르도 와인도 함께 나누어 마셨다. 엄마는 우리가 돈을 저축하지 않고 써재끼는 것을 비난하지 않았다. 다만 그 돈은 할머니가 살아 계신 동안만 받을 수 있는 연금보험이라는 것을 잊지 말라고 했다. 건강관리가 철저한 분이니 백 세까지도 넉넉히 사실 테지만 그래도 기한이 있다는 것을 잊지 말라고. 인철을 대하는 엄마의 태도는 전보다 한결 부드러워져

the afternoon. Incheol's with me, so don't worry."

She hesitated for a moment and asked, "What did you tell him about the money?"

I knew right away what she was asking me. "I told him the truth. It's not some huge secret, Mom. Incheol acted like he'd struck gold. You know what the first thing he said to me was? He was like, 'What did I dream about last night to deserve such a fortune?'"

Mom let out a weak laugh as though at a loss for words. But she sounded somewhat relieved.

Okay, that's great, she said and told me to get some rest before hanging up.

After I was discharge from the hospital, Incheol and I took the bus home. On the way back home, we talked about what we wanted to do if we really had five million won coming in every month. The first thing I wanted to do, I said, was to go on a trip. A spontaneous trip without any plans. A trip where I didn't have to think about the time I had left or the money, or have a return date in mind. A trip where I could go wherever my feet led me and unpack my luggage whenever I wanted to rest as much as I wanted. I would definite-

있었다. 헤어지기 전, 엄마는 지난 일은 미안했다고 자그마한 목소리로 말했다. 인철은 희게 웃으며 고개를 끄덕였다.

그다음 해 봄에 우리는 엄마와 외할머니를 모시고 제주도 여행을 다녀왔다. 그것은 인철의 생각이었다. 두 사람과 여행이라니, 영 내키지 않았지만 인철의 성화에 못 이겨 외할머니와 엄마에게 의향을 물었다. 둘 다 선뜻 좋다고 대답해서, 가슴이 철렁 내려앉았다.

"이제 어떻게 할 거야?"

"뭘, 재미있게 놀다 오는 거지. 꽃도 보고, 나무도 보고."

인철은 천진하게 말했다.

"두고 봐. 여행 내내 두 사람을 양쪽 어깨에 올리고 다녀야 할걸."

"너무 과장하지 마."

비행기에 오르는 순간부터 외할머니는 두통을 호소했다. 도착하자마자 먹은 전복 솥밥에서 이상한 냄새가 난다고 했고, 결국 한 숟가락 뜬 것이 얹혀서 약을 찾아 한참 시내를 헤매야 했다. 할머니는 이마에 손

ly avoid coffeeshops or restaurants or any other places with children. I would only go to clean and quiet places for adults. I was done with all the screaming, tattling, sulking, and giggling. So fed up with kids!

Incheol looked at me with a look of surprise.

"I like kids…" Then, after a moment's hesitation, he said, "But if I have five million won coming in every month, and I have no pressure to find a job… then I want to focus on writing again. For just one more year."

I nodded. "If we have a set income, then we'll be happy to do anything. We can get out of bed late, eat a pile of peanuts, goof around with our cat, and dance all night under the bridge. And who'll tell me I shouldn't?"

"I'm grateful to your grandmother," Incheol said with a smile. "It's been a long time since we've been able to have such pleasant thoughts. But it's not a small sum, and I'm not a hundred percent comfortable. You should think on it, and I won't object if you say no to the money."

At a bus stop near our home, an old lady with a cane boarded the bus, and the driver waited until she slowly walked through the bus to find a seat. After watching

을 얹고 8인승 승합차의 맨 뒤에 누워 있기만 했다. 한편 엄마는 처음부터 이상하리만치 기분이 좋았다. 엄마에게 새 남자친구가 생긴 것을 그날 처음 알았다. 음악학원의 소득세 신고 기간에 만난 대머리 세무사라고 했다. 엄마는 공항에서 내내 그와 속삭이며 통화하더니 비행기에서 내린 후에는 무슨 이유인지 티격태격했고, 전화를 끊고서는 무거운 얼굴로 입을 다물어버렸다. 계속해서 전화벨이 울리는데도 무시했다. 듣다 못한 할머니가 그럴 거면 휴대폰을 꺼놓으라고 뒷좌석에서 소리쳤다. 창밖으로 에메랄드빛 바다가 펼쳐지는데, 아무도 관심이 없었다. 운전대를 잡은 인철은 진땀을 흘리며 혼자 허공에 질문을 던지고, 실없이 웃었다.

늦은 오후, 우리는 가까스로 근방에서 제일 유명하다는 카페를 찾아 들어갔다. 남국풍의 밀짚 지붕이 멋스러운 카페였다. 색색깔의 옷을 입은 젊은 사람들이 바글바글했다. 마침 잡지사에서 취재를 왔는지 매장 한가운데 커다란 카메라가 세워져 있었다. 바다가 한눈에 보이는 테라스 쪽 자리에 앉으려는데, 카페 사장이 다가와서 우리를 훑어보더니 그곳은 '예약석'이라며 저지했다. 예약 손님이 있느냐고 되묻자 손님이 없어

her in silence, Incheol said, "Your grandmother... it must have been a hard life."

"Yeah, you're right," I agreed.

A sum of money that came in every month at no cost. Was it really possible? It turned out it was. Every month on the 10th, the money came in. Incheol said he wasn't fully comfortable taking the money, but pish posh. I felt no such thing. I waited anxiously for the 10th every month. The money was really useful. It was more than enough for us to move into a new apartment with a higher rent. I didn't go back to work at the cram school. Instead I stayed home, free from worldly cares, watching the flecks of dust floating in the sunlight. We bought and ate as much beef, fried chicken, tteokbokki, cherries, and grapefruits as we wanted. I bought a new pair of sneakers and signed up for a Pilates class. I split the money with Incheol, and he was also able to read and write all day without having to hold onto a regular job.

While eating dinner, watching TV, or taking a stroll through the streets at night, we impulsively set out on trips. It was like a children's game. A game where, as

도 비워둔다고 했다. 노인들이 있다고 차별하는 거냐, 나는 날카롭게 쏘아붙였다. 히피 펌을 한 여자 사장은 기막힌다는 얼굴로 나를 노려보더니 가게에서 나가달라고 했다. 가슴속에 차곡차곡 쌓아올린 장작 위로 화르륵 불이 붙는 기분이었다. 정신을 차리고 보니 나는 카페 한가운데서 고성을 내며 싸우고 있었다. 상대측에서 고소하겠다는 소리가 나왔을 때, 인철이 나를 들어 옮기다시피 하여 싸움이 일단락되었다. 한쪽 구석에서 외할머니와 엄마가 안절부절못하며 나를 기다리고 있었다. 그들은 내게 대체 뭐가 문제냐고 물었다. 나는 아무 말도 하지 않고 자리를 떴다. 호텔로 들어가 방에서 혼자 텔레비전을 보다가 일찍 잠자리에 들었다.

첫날의 소란 이후 2박 3일의 여정은 시간을 길게 늘인 것처럼 지루하게 흘렀다. 하늘은 내내 흐렸고, 바람이 많이 불었다. 관광지 어디에도 별 흥미가 없던 외할머니는 가파도에 있다는 청보리밭만큼은 꼭 가고 싶다고 했다. 너울성 파도로 연일 배가 뜨지 않다가 돌아가기 전날에야 겨우 운항 스케줄이 잡혔다. 외할머니는 스카프를 목에 친친 감고 배에 올랐다. 선내로 들어가자고 해도 꼼짝 않고 배의 후미에 서서 포말을 일으키

soon as someone mentioned a trip, you took as little time as possible to book the train tickets, pack the bags, open the door, and walk outside. As we mastered the game, it took less than five minutes for a word from our lips to become a reality. We no longer asked each other about how this kind of life was possible. It was like an inscrutable divine grace. At one end, however, was definitely an old woman who paid the price, and we had no choice but to talk about her on the 10th of every month—about the stigma of being a host of a disease, the deprivation of citizenship, isolation, demeaning and degrading of character, and random abortions and biological experiments. Our conversations were stilted, cut off by silences, and Incheol trembled. He stayed home alone and wrote. In the dark of the night, he turned on the desk lamp and sat with his back rounded, constantly writing something.

The following year, Incheol once again didn't win any of the annual spring literary competitions hosted by newspapers or other writing contests. In one competition, his work was named as one of the finalists, but it received a harsh criticism that it was "a story too

는 바닷길을 바라보았다.

　배로 이십 분도 가지 않아 도착한 그 작은 섬은 보리밭으로 가득 메워져 있었다. 연두색 보릿대가 휘청휘청 흔들리며 지평선 끝까지 펼쳐진 풍경이 장관이었다. 엄마는 선글라스를 끼고 배우처럼 포즈를 취했다. 우리는 낮은 의자에 나란히 앉아 처음으로 단체사진을 찍었다. 섬을 한 바퀴 돌고 나무 그늘 아래 휴게소에서 보리빵과 아이스크림을 먹었다. 외할머니는 꾸벅꾸벅 졸았다. 할머니의 스카프가 땅바닥으로 흘러내렸다. 엄마는 조용히 그것을 주워들었다. 세무사 아저씨랑 화해했냐고 묻자 피식 웃으며 그렇다고 대답했다. 우리는 별 볼거리도 없는 섬에서 한나절을 보낸 뒤 마지막 배를 타고 나왔다.

　여행의 마지막 밤 우리는 야외 수영장 한편에 마련된 바에서 맥주를 마셨다. 호텔 목욕탕에 다녀온 후 쉬겠다는 외할머니와 엄마를 설득해서 인철이 만든 자리였다. 수위가 낮은 온수풀이라 어린아이를 둔 부부들이 많았다. 외할머니는 오랫동안 그 풍경을 지켜보았다. 엄마는 인철과 짧고 긴 대화를 나누다 우스갯소리를 하기도 했다. 선선한 바람이 부는 밤, 검은 하늘에

trite and banal that it even overshadows great writing." Incheol said that he was going to stop writing. He said he had done enough, that he had no more regrets, and that he was grateful to everyone. It was as if he was giving an award acceptance speech. Both of us nearly cried. Then he received a phone call from one of the judges, who wanted to stage his play.

Incheol staged his first play at the biggest theater in Seoul. On the last day of the show, Mom came to the theater. After the play was over, all of us went to dinner together. She didn't say a word about the play, which was about a woman suffering from the Hansen's disease. Instead, she only asked about trivial stuff, like how old Incheol was when he first started writing plays, how many days it took to write a play, and how many hours a day he spent at his desk.

Mom ate an unusually large amount of food that night. She also shared a vintage Bordeaux wine she'd specially brought for us. She didn't criticize us for spending the money instead of saving up. She just told us that we shouldn't forget that the money was an annuity that we could only receive while Grandma was

키 큰 야자수가 끝도 없이 솟아 있었다. 어디선가 은은한 피아노 연주곡이 들렸다. 인철이 여행 내내 동분서주하며 만들고자 했던 유쾌한 분위기—나는 그것이 가능하지 않다고 단언했지만—가 감돌았다. 그날 밤 잠시간 어떤 친밀감이 우리 사이에 휘장처럼 드리웠다. 외할머니는 자신의 고향 이야기를 했다. 고향에 있었던 보리밭, 함께 자란 친구들, 그중 일찍 결혼한 친구의 딸, 해원. 머루처럼 검푸른 머리카락을 가진 여자아이. 인형처럼 작고 예뻤던 아이.

나는 이야기 속 해원이 친구의 딸이 아닌 외할머니의 딸이라는 것을 알고 있었다. 할머니는 내가 자신의 삶을 속속들이 다 알고 있다는 사실을 몰랐을 것이다. 엄마에게 준 돈이 결국 내게 흘러들어온다는 것도 몰랐을 것이다. 아니, 어쩌면 다 알고 있었을 것이다. 이제와서는 아무래도 상관없다는 생각이 든다.

여행에서 돌아온 뒤 나는 임신 사실을 확인했다. 어떻게 이런 일이, 어떻게? 인철과 나는 앵무새처럼 같은 말을 반복했다. 피임은 철저했고, 단 한 번 깜빡하는 실수도 없었다. 어떻게 이런 일이, 어떻게? 우리는 눈

still living—that since Grandma took good care of her health she would probably live to a hundred years old but still the money would stop coming in at some point. Mom was a lot more tender with Incheol. Before we parted, she apologized to him in a small voice, saying that she was sorry for what she did to him in the past. Incheol smiled brightly and accepted her apology.

In the spring of the following year, we went on a trip to Jeju Island with Mom and Grandma. It was Incheol's idea. I was very reluctant to travel with the two of them, but I could no longer stand him nagging me and eventually asked Grandma and Mom about going on a trip. Both of them readily answered that they would love to go, and my heart sank.

"What are we going to do now?"

Incheol said innocently, "What else? We're going to have fun, looking at flowers and trees."

"Just you watch. You will have to carry them on your shoulders the entire trip."

"Stop exaggerating."

From the moment we got on the plane, Grandma

만 마주치면 서로에게 물었다. 어쨌든 그런 일은 벌어졌다. 인철은 다시 유리 반지를 준비했는데 전처럼 그게 악질의 장난이라는 생각은 들지 않았다. 꼭 돈 때문은 아니겠지만 전과 달라진 거라곤 매달 들어오는 돈, 그 돈밖에 없었다. 그러니까 그 돈이 있어서 마음이 바뀐 것이다. 우리는 경기도 외곽의 소형 아파트로 이사한 뒤 결혼했다.

인철은 근근하게 희곡 작업을 계속해나갔다. 앞이 보이지 않기는 전과 마찬가지였고, 이것이 광맥인지 아닌지도 여전히 확신할 수 없었으나 더이상 계속해야 하나 말아야 하나 망설이지 않았다. 그는 매일 썼고, 다음 작품 역시 무대에 올릴 기회를 얻었다. 그 경력으로 제법 규모가 큰 입시학원의 국어 강사로 자리잡게 되었다. 나 역시 과외 강사 자리를 구해 다시 일을 시작했다. 딸아이가 태어난 후 우리는 미약한 우울증과 불면증, 허리 디스크를 나눠 가졌다. 아이의 이름은 해원으로 지었다. 해원의 돌잔치 때 외할머니는 처음으로 우리집에 왔다.

"이 이름이 예뻐서 저희가 가졌어요. 괜찮죠?"

"그거야 너희 마음이지. 너희 딸이니까."

complained of a headache. She carped about the abalone rice pot she ordered when we landed on Jeju Island, saying that it had a strange smell. The single spoonful of it that she ate ended up giving her indigestion that we had to roam the downtown area to look for medicine. Grandma lay in the back of the eight-seater van with an arm across her forehead. Meanwhile, Mom seemed to be in a strangely happy mood from the start. That day, I found out that she had a boyfriend. She said he was a bald tax accountant whom she met while filing taxes for her music academy. The entire time at the airport, she was on the phone with him, talking in whispers. But after she got off the plane she quarreled with him for one reason or another. With a grim look on her face, she hung up the phone and stopped talking. She continued to ignore her ringing phone. Unable to stand listening to the ringing phone, Grandma shouted at Mom from the backseat to turn off the cell phone if she wasn't going to answer it. An emerald sea stretched outside the window, but no one seemed to care. At the steering wheel, Incheol was sweating hard, throwing questions into the air and smiling for no reason.

외할머니는 특유의 무심한 얼굴로 우리를 보며 말했다. 해원은 노란 저고리에 빨간 치마 한복을 입고 금박의 굴레를 썼다. 지루한 돌잡이 과정을 할머니와 엄마, 나만 즐거워하며 바라보았다. 우리는 손뼉을 치며 웃었다. 인철이 해원과 우리의 사진을 찍어주었다. 나는 그 사진을 인화해서 거실 벽에 걸어놓았다.

해원이 두 돌을 맞을 무렵 외할머니는 돌아가셨다. 갑작스러운 당뇨합병증이었다. 누구보다 까다롭게 식단을 조절하고 건강을 관리해온 할머니였기에 모두가 놀랐다. 어느 날 저녁 할머니는 의자에서 일어나다가 뒤로 넘어졌고, 그때부터 말을 어눌하게 더듬었다. 급성 뇌경색이라고 했다. 병원에 입원한 지 세 달 만에 할머니는 눈을 감았다. 마치 그러기로 계획되어 있던 것처럼 죽음의 과정은 신속했다.

엄마는 점심때가 다 되어 외숙부의 집에서 나왔다. 외숙부가 원하는 대로 통장 거래 내역까지 일일이 확인시켜준 뒤였다. 아무 증거도 찾아내지 못한 외숙부는 연신 탄식했고(그 많은 돈을 대체 어디다 쓰셨을까), 엄마는 그를 위로했고(원래 속을 알 수 없는 양반이잖아), 그럼

Late in the afternoon, we managed to find one of the most popular cafés in the area. It was a stylish café with a southern-style straw roof. There were crowds of young people in colorful clothes. A large camera stood in the middle of the store, possibly from a magazine that was doing a story on this café. We were about to head out to the terrace with the view of the sea when the café owner approached us. She scanned us up and down and stopped us from sitting down, saying that the table was reserved. When I asked if someone had already reserved the table, she said that they leave the table unoccupied even if it wasn't reserved. Are you stopping us because you're discriminating against old people?, I snapped at her. The café owner with a hippie perm looked at me as if she couldn't believe what I was saying and asked me to leave. It felt like she'd lit a fire on top of the firewood that had been piled up neatly in my chest. When I got back to my senses, I found myself screaming at her in the middle of the café. When the owner said that she was going to file a lawsuit, Incheol practically lifted me up and removed me from the café, and the fight was finally over. Mom and Grand-

에도 그의 타는 듯한 마음은 진정되지 않았다. 할머니가 돌아가시기 전 연금보험의 남은 원금마저 융통하여 쓴 사실이 드러난 것이다. 남은 돈은 한 푼도 없었다. 두 사람은 상속받을 것이 아무것도 없다는 것을 확인한 후 헤어졌다. 엄마는 집에서 나오다가 현관 앞 상자에 담긴 몇 가지 물건을 보았다. 외숙부는 지친 목소리로 다 버릴 것들이니 가져가려면 가져가라고 했다. 엄마는 그 안에서 스카프를 집어들었다.

나는 외할머니의 스카프를 맨 엄마를 차에 태웠다. 밥을 먹으러 가자고 했더니 엄마는 시계를 흘긋 보고, 그냥 터미널로 가자고 했다.

"해원이도 보지 않고 갈 거예요?"

"응, 이 차 놓치면 다음 차는 저녁에나 있단 말이야."

엄마는 얼마 전부터 대머리 세무사와 동거를 시작했다. 결혼보다 '더 나쁜' 동거를 택할 수밖에 없는 애정의 임계점을 넘어선 것이다. 나는 그 남자에 대해 아무것도 묻지 않았다. 부디 그가 좋은 사람이기를, 그래서 엄마가 다시는 한밤중에 짐을 싸지 않아도 되기를 바랄 뿐이었다.

터미널에서 우리는 버스표를 끊고 우동을 먹었다. 엄

ma were waiting nervously for me in a corner. They asked me what the hell was wrong with me. I left without a word. I headed to the hotel, watched TV alone in my room, and went to bed early.

After the commotion on the first day, the next two nights and three days went by tediously as if time had lengthened. The sky was overcast the entire time, and there was a lot of wind. Grandma, who had no interest in any of the tourist destinations, said that she really wanted to go see the green barley fields on Gapa Island. The ferry was canceled due to swelling waves, and it was finally opened the day before the last day of our trip. Grandma wrapped a scarf around her neck and climbed onto the ferry. Even when I asked her come inside, she remained standing at the aft, looking out at the foamy sea path.

The tiny island that we arrived in less than twenty minutes by boat was covered in barley fields. The yellow-green barley stalks swaying to and fro as they stretched out to the end of the horizon—it was a simply spectacular sight. Mom put on her sunglasses and posed like an actress. All of us sat side by side on a low

마는 우동이 아무 맛이 없다고 투덜거렸다. 우동을 다 먹고도 시간이 조금 남아서 우리는 자판기 커피를 뽑아 벤치에 앉았다.

"할머니 장례식에 그 여자가 왔던 거 아니? 해원."

나는 깜짝 놀라 엄마를 바라보았다.

"어떻게?"

"내가 찾았지. 나 말고 누가 있니?"

엄마가 피식 웃었다.

"외할머니 마지막에 병원 계실 때 찾았어. 그리고 만났지. 네 외숙부 모르게."

"어땠어요?"

"뭘 어때, 울고불고 난리였지. 완전히 신파 드라마. 돌아가실 때까지 몇 번 더 만났어."

엄마는 손에 든 종이컵을 바라보았다.

"딸을 찾아줘서 고마웠는지, 나한테도 엄청 잘해줬어. 천사가 따로 없더라. 마지막에는 꼭 다른 사람처럼 보였어. 탈이라도 벗은 것처럼…… 나한테 너무 매몰찼다고, 평생 다정하게 대해주지 못해서 미안하다고 사과하더라."

엄마는 고개를 숙였다.

bench and took our first group photo. After a walk around the island, we ate barley bread and ice cream at a rest area in the shade of a tree. Grandma dozed. Her scarf slid down to the ground. Mom quietly picked it up. When I asked her if she had made up with the tax accountant, she grinned and replied, Yes. We spent the entire day on this tiny island with little to see and took the last ferry out of the island.

On the last night of our trip, we drank beer at the outdoor poolside bar at our hotel. It was Incheol's idea—he persuaded Mom and Grandma to come out even though they said they wanted to go to the hotel sauna and then head back to their room to rest. There were many couples with small children at the pool as the water was shallow and heated. Grandma watched the scene for a long time. Mom had short and long conversations with Incheol, and even made a few jokes. On that cool windy night, tall palm trees rose endlessly into the black sky. We could hear soft piano music coming from somewhere. There was a pleasant vibe, which I had declared was impossible but Incheol had been trying hard to create throughout the trip. For a brief

"사과해도 소용없다고 했지. 그리고 물어봤어. 고아
원에 왜 한 번도 안 찾아왔느냐고. 한 번만이라도 찾아
와서 잘 참으라고, 곧 데리러 온다고 말해줬으면 좋지
않았겠냐고. 그랬더니 그 양반 뭐라고 했는지 알아?"

엄마는 바람 빠진 소리를 내며 웃었다.

"기억이 안 난대. 그 시절의 일은 전부 다 잊어버렸
대. 자기는 열 명분의 인생을 산 것 같다고…… 늘 분주
하고 너무 많이 피곤했다고, 등이 휘도록 피곤했다고
그러더라."

"뭔지 알 것 같아."

"네가 알긴 뭘 알아."

엄마는 어린아이를 꾸짖듯 말했다.

버스 시간이 다 되자, 엄마는 가뿐하게 자리에서 일
어났다. 라 캄파넬라, 벨이 울렸고 엄마는 전화를 받으
면서 버스에 올랐다. 남자의 부드러운 목소리가 희미
하게 들렸다.

창가 자리에 앉은 엄마는 내게 손을 흔들었다. 스카
프를 목에 친친 두른 엄마가 외할머니와 놀랍도록 닮
아 보여 나는 잠시 숨을 삼켰다.

터미널에서 차를 돌려 집으로 가는 길, 나는 부러 전

moment that night, something like intimacy hung like a veil over all four of us. Grandma told us a story about her hometown. The barley fields, the friends she grew up with, and Haewon, the daughter of her friend who married young. A girl with dark, dark blue hair like mulberries. A petite little girl who was pretty like a doll.

I knew that Haewon in Grandma's story was not her friend's daughter, but her own. Grandma probably didn't know that I knew about her life in such detail. She wouldn't even have known that the money she gave Mom ended up coming to me. Or perhaps she'd known everything. At this point, it doesn't really matter.

After we returned home from the trip, I found out I was pregnant. How did this happen, how? Incheol and I parroted the same words. We were thorough with protection, and we never forgot to use contraception, not even once. How did this happen, how? We asked each other whenever our eyes met. In any event, what happened was what happened. Incheol gave me the glass ring again, but I didn't think it was a bad joke this time. It wasn't necessarily because of the money, but

에 인철과 내가 살던 연립주택가를 지나갔다. 좁은 골목을 통과하는데 과거의 한 부분으로 돌아간 것 같은 기분이 들었다. 나는 그곳에서 겪었던 가장 즐거운 일과 가장 고통스러운 일을 떠올려보았다. 어느 집에서 미숙한 피아노 연주 소리가 흘러나왔다. 꿈인 듯 아득한 소리였다. 그 소리는 영원히 계속될 것 같았지만 마침내 멈추었고, 그러자 골목에 남은 것은 침묵뿐이었다.

the only thing that was different from the time of his first proposal was the money coming in every month. So, my heart had changed because of that money. We moved into a small apartment on the outskirts of Gyeonggi Province and got married.

Incheol continued to grind away at writing his plays. Just as before, there was no guaranteed future, and he still wasn't sure if he would strike a lode with what he was writing, but he didn't hesitate whether to continue or not. He wrote every day, and he got a chance to stage his next play as well. Thanks to his work, he found himself a stable job as a Korean language instructor at a fairly large college entrance exam prep school. I also found a job as a tutor and started working again. After our daughter was born, the two of us came to share mild depression, insomnia, and herniated disks. We named our girl Haewon. For Haewon's first birthday party, Grandma came to our house for the first time.

"We named her Haewon because it's such a pretty name," I told her. "You're okay with it, right?"

"That's up to you," Grandma said with her typical aloof look on her face.

Haewon wore a yellow jeogori and a red skirt and donned a gold head piece. Only Grandma, Mom, and I watched with the boring doljabi as Haewon stretched out her hand to grab one of the items laid out in front of her that would determine her future fortune. We clapped our hands and laughed out loud. Incheol took pictures of us with Haewon. I printed one out and hung it in our living room.

Grandma passed away around Haewon's second birthday. It was from sudden diabetic complication. Everyone was surprised because she had been stricter than anyone else in controlling her diet and taking care of her health. One evening prior to her death, Grandma stood up from her chair and fell backward, and she began to slur her words. They said it was an acute cerebral infarction. Three months after she was admitted to the hospital, Grandma closed her eyes forever. The process of her death was swift as if it had been planned.

Mom came out of Uncle's apartment around lunch time. It was after she'd shown him all of her bankbook transactions one by one, as he wanted. Unable to find any trace of the money, Uncle apparently lamented over and over again (Where could she possibly have spent that much money?), and Mom comforted him (She was a hard nut to crack—you could never tell what she was thinking). Yet the desperation in his heart did not subside. Because he'd found out that Grandma had taken out and used the remaining principal of her annuity before her death. There was not a single penny left. Mom and Uncle parted after confirming that they had nothing to inherit. As Mom came out of Uncle's apartment, she noticed some items in a box by the front door. In a weary voice, Uncle told her to take anything she wanted since he was going to throw them out anyway. Mom took Grandma's scarf from the box.

Mom got into my car, wearing Grandma's scarf around her neck.

I said, "Let's grab something to eat." But she looked at her watch and said she wanted to straight to the bus terminal.

"You're not even going to see Haewon before you go?"

"No, if I miss this bus, the next one doesn't come until late in the evening."

A little while ago Mom moved in with the bald tax accountant. She'd crossed the critical point of affection to choose cohabitation, which was, in her words, worse than marriage. I didn't ask anything about her boyfriend. I only hoped that he was a good man, so that she wouldn't have to pack her bags in the middle of the night again.

At the bus terminal, Mom bought her ticket, and we had some udon noodles. She complained that the udon was tasteless. After we finished our lunch, we still had a little more time, so we bought two cups of vending machine coffee and sat down on the bench.

"Did you know that she came to the funeral? Haewon, I mean."

I turned to look at her in surprise. "How?"

"I found her," she giggled. "Who else would do it? I found her when your grandma was in the hospital in her last days. And they met. Your uncle has no idea."

"How did it go?"

"How do you think? They cried and cried. It was like watching a melodrama. They met a few more times until she died."

Mom looked down at the paper cup in her hand. "I think she was thankful that I'd found her daughter for her, because she was really nice to me too in her last days. She was practically an angel. At the end, she almost seemed like a different person. Like she'd shed a layer of skin or something. She apologized, told me she was sorry for having been so cold to me, for not being more affectionate all my life."

Mom hung her head and continued, "I said there was no use for an apology. And I asked her. Asked her why she never even came to see me once at the orphanage. Wouldn't it have been better for her to come see me at least once, to tell me to wait for her, that she'd come back for me. You know what she said to me then?"

Mom laughed, letting out a sound like air coming out of a tire. "She said she doesn't remember. She has no memory of that time at all. She said that it felt like she'd lived ten lives. She was always too busy and too exhausted, too drained."

"I think I know what she meant."

"What do you know?" Mom told me off, as if she were scolding a child.

When it was nearly time for her bus to leave, Mom got up lightly on her feet. "La Campanella"—her cell phone rang, and she answered the phone as she boarded the bus. I could hear the faint sound of a man's soft voice.

Mom sat by a window and waved at me. With the scarf around her neck, she looked so much like Grandma that it took my breath away for a moment.

On the way home from the bus terminal, I decided to drive by the townhouse where Incheol and I used to live together. As I passed through the narrow alley, I felt as though I'd returned to a part of my past. I tried to recall the happiest and the most painful experiences I'd had there. I heard the sound of an untrained musician playing the piano from somewhere. It sounded faint, like in a dream. It seemed to go on forever, but it finally ended, and all that was left in the alley was silence.

창작노트
Writer's Note

질병과 돈, 그리고 은총에 대한 이야기를 하고 싶다고 생각하며 이 소설을 썼습니다. 10년 전의 저는 믿지 않았던 것들입니다. 시간이 얼마나 빠르게 흐르는지, 우리가 진실이라고 믿는 것들이 얼마나 우습게 변해버리는지를 보면 놀랍습니다. 10년 후의 저는 또 지금 제가 믿지 않는 무엇인가에 대해 쓰고 있을지 모릅니다. 부디 그러하기를 바랍니다. 이 상을 주신 것은 더 이상 저이기를 부끄러워하지 말라는 뜻으로, 시시각각 깊어지고 넓어지라는 격려의 뜻으로 알겠습니다. 미숙한 저를 믿어주신 심사위원 선생님들께 감사드립니다. 충만한 기억을 오랫동안 간직하고, 두려움 없이 정진하겠습니다.

I wrote this short fiction, thinking that I wanted to talk about disease, money, and grace. These were things that I didn't believe in a decade ago. It is amazing to see how fast time flies, and how what we believe to be true turns into something laughable. Ten years from now, I might be writing about something that today's me do not believe in. In fact, I hope I do. I accept this award as a token of encouragement, that I should no longer be ashamed of myself, and that my thoughts should grow deeper and broader every moment. I am grateful to the judges of this award who believed in an inexperienced writer like myself. I will cherish this abounding memory for a lomg time and devote myself to writing, undaunted.

해설
Commentary

유기(遺棄)에서 해원(解冤)의 역사로

김보경 (문학평론가)

이 소설은 3대 모녀의 이야기로, 세 모녀는 각각 한센병력이 있는 외할머니, 그녀로부터 버림받았던 어린 시절의 기억을 잊지 못하고 살아가는 엄마, 그리고 엄마와 자신에게 냉랭하기 그지없었던 외할머니로부터 상처를 입고 "피부가 녹아내리는 병에 걸려서 사회로부터 배척당했던 한 무리의 사람들" 중 한 명이 외할머니라는 사실에도 별다른 감흥 없이 무심할 뿐인 화자에 해당한다. 한센인을 향한 사회적 억압과 폭력으로부터 자기 자신을 지키는 일만으로도 급급해 사랑하는 가족마저 버려야 했던 외할머니는 정작 그 사실로 가족들에게 이해받지 못하고 지독한 애증과 원망의 대상

From the history of abandonment to resolution

Kim Bokyung (Literary Critic)

This short story centers on three generations of women—the grandmother who has Hansen's disease, the mother who lives with the memory of being abandoned by the grandmother in her childhood, and the narrator who, having been hurt by the grandmother's cold attitude toward her and her mother in time of need, feels indifferent about the fact that her grandmother belonged to a group of people who were "shunned by society because of a skin-melting disease." Intent on protecting her ownself from the social oppression and violence against people with Hansen's disease, the grandmother abandoned her own daughter, which

이 되는 인물이다. 보통 3세대 인물의 시선에서 쓰인 3
대 서사는 역사라는 지도 위에서 자기 정체성을 탐색
하거나 위치를 설정하는 작업이라 할 수 있을 텐데, 이
소설의 경우 화자의 위치는 지도 바깥에 존재한다. 화
자는 외할머니의 삶을 "으스스한 분위기의 미국 드라
마 소재로나 어울리는 이야기" 정도로 소원하게 느끼
며 자기와는 무관한 건조한 사실로 여겨왔기 때문이다.

그 역사의 구체적인 내용을 살펴보면 이는 버림받는
여성들의 역사로 요약된다. 외할머니는 한센병에 걸
리자 당시 남편이었던 자에 의해 죽음을 권유받게 되
는데, 이를 피해 결국 어린 딸을 남겨두고 한센인 수용
소가 있는 섬으로 도망쳐 가게 된다. 한센인들은 그 섬
에서 "실질적인 전염력을 가지지 않음에도 오해와 억
측만으로 린치를 당하고 격리 수용 당하고, 죽는 날까
지 가족들을 만나지 못하"도록 강제되거나 단종수술
을 받는 등 사회로부터 철저히 버림받고 초법적 인권
유린이 허용되는 예외 상태에 놓여왔다. 이처럼 가족
과 사회로부터 버림받은 외할머니는 그 섬 안의 교회
에서 일하는 전쟁고아를 만나 그와 결혼하게 되고 섬
을 탈출해 한센인 격리촌인 협동농장에 들어가게 된

in turn made her resented and never understood by her family, who love yet also hate her. Narratives spanning three generations of a family told from the view of a character from the third generation often focus on the character's exploration of her own identity or her position in the map of her family history. However, the narrator of this short story exists outside of that map. She feels distant from her grandmother and considers the grandmother's life a "story you might come across in an American TV show with an eerie vibe" and a dull fact that has nothing to do with her.

When we look at the specific details of the narrator's family history, it can be summarized as the history of abandoned women. After the narrator's grandmother discovers that she has Hansen's disease, her husband advises her to kill herself. To live, she leaves her baby girl behind and escapes to an island that serves as a community for Hansen's disease patients. On the island, people with Hansen's disease are left completely neglected by society with rampant human rights violations, as they are "lynched, quarantined, and banned from seeing their families their entire lives," and even

다. 그런데 이때 두 자식을 모두 데려갈 수 없었던 외할머니는 아들만 데려가고 딸은 고아원에 보내기로 선택한다. 악착같이 돈을 벌어 농장 생활을 청산할 때에 이르러서야 딸을 다시 불러들이고 양육에 있어서 지원을 아끼지 않았지만, 외할머니의 딸 그러니까 화자의 엄마는 고아원에 자신이 버려졌다는 기억을 잊지 못하고 자신을 버렸음에도 별 가책을 느끼지 못하는 것 같이 보이는 외할머니에 대한 원한과 애증을 품고 산다.

화자 역시도 이러한 역사의 일부로 존재한다. 경제적으로 살림이 어려워지자, 화자의 아버지가 엄마를 향해 폭력을 일삼게 된 것이 계기가 되어 이들은 아버지로부터 도망쳐 나오게 된다. 그런데 그로부터 도망쳐 온 엄마와 화자가 외할머니에게로 당도했을 때, 그녀는 이들을 따뜻하게 맞이하기는커녕 그에게 돌아가라며 "맞고 사는 여자들은 다 이유가 있다"는 말로 엄마와 화자에게 돌이킬 수 없는 상처를 남긴다. 외할머니의 이 같은 말은 자기 존재가 그나마 남편으로 상징되는 가부장제의 울타리 안에서 보호받을 수 있었던 경험과 일평생 축적된 내면화된 자기혐오 및 여성혐오가 뒤섞여 나온 말이었겠지만, 그 사연이야 어찌 됐든 이

forcibly sterilized due to misunderstanding and spec-
ulation about the disease despite the fact that they are
not contagious. Abandoned by her own family and society, the grandmother remarries a man, who grew up
as a war orphan and works for the only church on the
island, and together they have two children. Eventually they flee the island to go live at a collective farm for
Hansen's disease patients. Yet, unable to take both of
their children to the farm, the grandmother takes the
older boy and sends her younger daughter to an orphanage. She works furiously on the farm to make
money, and once she has made enough to leave the
farm she brings her daughter back from the orphanage. Once the family becomes whole again, she spares
no expense to raise her daughter, but her daughter—
the narrator's mother—resents her for seeming to feel
no remorse or regret about abandoning her in an orphanage.

The narrator exists as part of this history. When the
narrator's family begins to struggle financially, her father beats her mother, which prompts the narrator
and her mother to run away from him. They go to the

말은 모녀에게 이해될 수도 용서될 수도 없는 말로 각인된다. 외할머니의 이러한 매정함에 화자는 "외할머니를 절대로 용서하지 않겠다"고, 만약 엄마가 그녀를 용서한다면 자신은 그런 엄마를 용서하지 않겠다고 다짐하기에 이른다. 이 같은 원망은 화자가 외할머니와 자기 삶을 분리하는 감정적 기제로 작동하며 화자에게 외할머니의 내력이 외할머니의 말이나 행동을 이해하는 데 도움을 주는 요소가 아니라 그저 "뜬구름 같은 얘기"로만 느껴지도록 하는 데 일조해왔다.

이런 화자가 외할머니의 삶을 곱씹고 자기와 긴밀히 연결된 존재로서 생각하게 되는 것은 외할머니의 보험금을 받게 되면서부터다. 외할머니가 일했던 곳인 한센인 협동농장의 대표가 뒷돈을 받고 헐값으로 땅을 팔았다는 사실이 드러난 후 진행된 법정 다툼에서 외할머니는 적극적으로 소송에 참여했던 사람 중 한 명이다. 그리고 외할머니는 소송으로 받게 된 보상금으로 연금보험을 들어놓는데, 이를 유산의 명목으로 자기 딸에게 주고, 이는 화자에게 돌아온 것이다. 화자와 그의 애인 인철은 경제적으로 궁핍함에 시달리던 차돈을 받지 않을 수 없었고, 매달 이를 받게 되며 안정을

narrator's grandmother for help, but instead of welcoming them with open arms, she inflicts irrevocable wounds on them by saying, "There's a reason some women get beaten by their husbands." The grandmother's words must have been a result of her own experience of finding protection within patriarchy under her second husband, as well as self-hatred and misogyny she'd internalized throughout her life. However, regardless of her situation, those words are unacceptable and unforgivable to the narrator and her mother. Her grandmother's cold attitude leads the narrator to vow to "never forgive Grandma" and also to not forgive her own mother if she ever forgives the grandmother. Such resentment works as an emotional mechanism that allows the narrator to dissociate her life from her grandmother's, which has contributed to the narrator's attitude of seeing her grandmother's past as a tall tale rather than as a factor that helps her understand her grandmother's words and actions.

The narrator comes to contemplate her grandmother's life and think of her as someone who is closely related to herself, however, when she begins to receive

누릴 수 있게 되자 이 보험금을 "이상한 은총" 같다고 느낀다. 화자와 인철이 받게 된 것은 보험금만이 아니다. 이 은총의 뒤에는 "분명 대가를 지불한 늙은이"가 있었기 때문이다. 이들은 매달 돈이 들어올 때마다 "질병의 숙주라는 오명, 시민권의 박탈, 격리 생활, 인격 비하와 모멸, 무작위로 행해진 낙태와 생체실험에 대해" 대화를 나누고 희곡을 쓰는 인철은 외할머니와 관련된 이야기를 써 작품을 올리게 되기도 한다.

이러한 보상금은 단순히 금전적인 의미만 가지고 있지 않다. 우선 이는 외할머니 자신에게는 그의 불우했던 삶에 대한 보상에 해당하며, 두 번째로 엄마에게는 외할머니가 자신의 오래된 부채감을 해소하고 엄마에게 조금이나마 용서를 구하려는 용서의 표시이기도 하고, 마지막으로 화자에게 이는 외할머니가 살아온 삶의 유산을 의미한다. 이러한 유산을 받아 든 화자는 외할머니의 삶을 되돌아보게 되고 그 과정에서 외할머니의 삶과 자기의 삶을 적극적으로 연루시키며 그를 이해할 실마리를 얻게 된다. 또한 이 보상금을 통해 엄마는 외할머니를 용서하지는 못할망정 적어도 그의 삶을 이해해보려는 기회를 갖게 된다. 그렇게 엄마는 외할머니가 처음 집에서 도망

her grandmother's annuity payouts. The grandmother was one of the active participants in the lawsuit against the manager of the collective farm that she had been a member of after people learn that he took a bribe and sold the farm for a bargain. With the money she won from the lawsuit, the grandmother signed up for an annuity. When the monthly payouts start, she gives the money to her daughter—the narrator's mother—in the name of inheritance, and the mother, in turn, gives the money to her own daughter, the narrator. Faced with financial hardship, the narrator and her boyfriend, Incheol, cannot refuse the money, and soon they feel as though the payouts are "inscrutable divine grace" as this regular income provides them with financial stability. The payouts are not the only things that the narrator and Incheol receive, as this divine grace came from an "old woman who paid the price." On the days the money comes in, they talk about the "stigma of being a host of a disease, the deprivation of citizenship, isolation, demeaning and degrading of character, and random abortions and biological experiments." Incheol, an aspiring playwright, writes a play about the narra-

칠 때 그가 버렸던 딸 해원을 되찾아주어, 외할머니가 죽기 전에 그가 해원(解冤)할 수 있는 기회를 선물하기에 이른다. 소설의 마지막 대목에서 화자와 인철이 자신들의 아이에게 '해원'이라는 이름을 붙이는 일 역시 이러한 해원의 시도로서, 이는 그들 나름의 방식으로 외할머니의 삶을 위로하고 기억하기 위한 시도로 읽힌다. 이러한 과정을 통해 화자는 외할머니와 엄마, 그리고 자기 자신에게로 이어지는 역사를 받아들이며 모계의 역사라는 지도 위에 설 수 있게 된다. 소설에는 이제 이 지도 위에 유기와 원한만이 아닌 '해원'의 역사가 쓰이게 될 것이라는 사실이 암시된다. 「지난밤 내 꿈에」는 바로 그 해원의 역사가 쓰일 수 있는 조건이 무엇인지 묻는다.

tor's grandmother, which is successfully staged.

The payouts, therefore, have more than monetary significance. To the grandmother, these payouts are compensation for her unfortunate past; to the mother, they are an apology from the grandmother who wants to clear her debt to her daughter for abandoning her as a child and ask for her forgiveness; and to the narrator, they are the legacy of her grandmother's life. With her grandmother's legacy in her hands, the narrator looks back on her grandmother's life, and while doing so she discovers the intricate connection between her own life and her grandmother's life and finds clues that help understand her grandmother. Moreover, the payouts give the mother a chance to understand the grandmother if not forgive her. Eventually, the mother finds Haewon (whose name is homonymous with the Korean word meaning "resolution of embitterment"), the grandmother's daughter from her first marriage she had left behind when she went to the island for Hansen's disease patients, presenting an opportunity for the grandmother to "haewon," or resolve her embittered feelings. Toward the end of the short story, the narrator and Incheol also name their daughter Haewon, which seems to be an attempt to resolve the embitterment that the narrator had felt toward her grandmother and to offer consolation and remember her grandmother's life. Through this process, the narrator comes to accept the history that continues from her grandmother and her mother down to herself, and positions herself on the map of matrilineal history. The story hints at the fact that the history of resolution will be written on this map, following the history of abandonment and resentment. In this way, "Last Night, In My Dream" asks about the conditions that are necessary for the history of resolution to be written.

비평의 목소리
Critical Acclaim

우리가 한국 현대사를 분노와 미움 없이 끌어안고 어쩌면 감히 화해할 수 있을지도 모르겠다는 희망을 받았다. 그 과정이 자연스럽고 따뜻했다.

장강명(소설가)

여러 삶의 내력을 징검다리 건너듯 건너다 보면 각자 짊어진 삶의 무게와 애틋한 마음들이 뭉클하다.

전성태(소설가)

오랜 시간 쌓인 공동체 내의 혐오와 상처를 통해 오히려 삶의 지속 가능성을 발견하고 믿는, 탁월한 조정자이자 주체인 여성 캐릭터의 힘이 압도적인 작품이다.

강영숙(소설가)

한센병력을 지닌 할머니로부터 시작된 여성 3대의 이야기를 통하여 상처와 회한이라는 결코 간단치 않은 삶의 진실을 형상화한 명편이다.

이경재(평론가)

I glimpsed hope that we might be able to embrace modern Korean history without anger and hatred and perhaps dare to reconcile with it. The process of doing so in this story was natural and heartwarming

Chang Kang-myoung (novelist)

As you cross the history of various lives as if you were crossing a river on stepping-stones, the weight of each character's life and longing stirs your heart.

Jeon Sung-tae (novelist)

This compelling work shows the power of female characters who are excellent mediators and agents of their own lives as they discover and believe in the sustainability of life through the hatred and wounds that have collected within a community over a long time.

Kang Young-sook (novelist)

This short story is a masterpiece that embodies the never-simple truth of lives—scars and remorse—through the story of three generations of women, starting with a grandmother who has Hansen's disease.

Lee Kyung-jae (Literary Critic)

K-픽션 032
지난밤 내 꿈에

2023년 3월 14일 초판 1쇄 발행

지은이 정한아 | 옮긴이 스텔라 김 | 펴낸이 김재범
기획위원 정은경, 전성태, 이경재
인쇄·제책 굿에그커뮤니케이션 | 종이 한솔PNS
펴낸곳 (주)아시아 | 출판등록 2006년 1월 27일 제406-2006-000004호
주소 경기도 파주시 회동길 445
전화 031.944.5058 | 팩스 070.7611.2505
메일 bookasia@hanmail.net
ISBN 979-11-5662-173-7(set) | 979-11-5662-625-1(04810)
값은 뒤표지에 있습니다.

K-Fiction 032
Last Night, In My Dream

Written by Chung Han-ah | Translated by Stella Kim
Published by ASIA Publishers
Address 445, Hoedong-gil, Paju-si, Gyeonggi-do, Korea
Tel. (8231).944.5058 | Fax. 070.7611.2505
E-mail bookasia@hanmail.net
First published in Korea by ASIA Publishers 2023
ISBN 979-11-5662-173-7(set) | 979-11-5662-625-1(04810)